The Day After Yesterday

Karli M Donalson

Colorful Crow Publishing

Chapter One

Today

It was raining the night he left for good. Large drops of water pelting against the tin roof left behind a melody of sadness. I don't remember much about the night's events that led him out of our home; the door slamming behind him. It was so typical of him; running away from conflict. He had done it so many times. I expected he would return after a few days in a hotel with only the small bag of clothes he kept packed for nights like these. Two weeks later, I would be served divorce papers that told me he wasn't coming home. My mother stood in the corner of the room, staring at the wall, completely oblivious to what was going on. I wasn't sad he was gone. I was sad about the time that had passed with him there. I was watching the days pass, one by one, in anticipation of my 40th birthday; too old to start over.

"It's time to feed the children."

Silence broken, I turned to face my mother. In her hands was evidence she had been peeling away at the yellowing wallpaper she so often stared at. I didn't feel like playing her games but knew if I didn't, I would pay for it later.

"I'll set the table."

She entered the den and dug through a wooden chest nestled in between a bookcase and a small gas heater. As she pulled each one from the quilt stuffed into the bottom, she called them by name.

"Sue.... such a sweet girl."

She tossed her to the ground behind her.

I really liked Sue. She had a big sewn-on smile that trailed up her cheeks, ending at pink painted-on dimples.

"Georgie, I hope you haven't been picking on the girls again."

I listened to her speak to each one as if, at any moment, they would respond. After a few minutes, she entered the kitchen and placed the handful of them into chairs. She straightened their dresses and tied on imaginary bibs. I found it ironic that I was helping my mother raise fictitious children while never knowing the joy of having real ones.

Ben never was interested in having children. I knew before I married him he was more interested in chasing dreams and attaining goals than in reproducing. I still dreamed. I thought maybe one day he would feel the weight of the future coming at him with no one to pass along the family name to. He needed an heir to his self-made fortune, right? I was wrong.

"I'll be taking everything I have with me when I go."

I thought he was referring to death, but throughout our divorce, I discovered he meant he would take everything he owned with him then, too.

The further we got in life, the less we interacted, and it is quite difficult to make babies without interacting.

"The babies are all crying."

The persistence in my mother's voice told me she was genuinely concerned for their well-being, and for a moment, I imagined her concern for me as a baby, what it must have been like to lie in her arms and listen to her sing. I was now left with an empty shell of her being that I watched care for cotton-stuffed children each and every day.

"Tomato soup is ready," I called out, hoping she had an appetite. She hardly ate anymore.

After no response, I headed into the living room to find her. She was sitting on the sofa, picking at imaginary lint. I watched her for a moment; her boney fingers grasping at nothing. After several picks, she leaned over the arm of the couch and released the little bits of nothing onto the floor. She watched as they floated down and landed on the carpet. I tried to imagine life in her world; her completely false, unfathomable world.

"Mom, lunch is ready. And the children are hungry." She looked at me as though I had spoken to her in a foreign language.

"I don't have children, silly. My bearing days are long gone."

This was nothing out of the ordinary for us. It was our new normal. I returned to the dining room alone and put away all of her baby dolls before setting aside the bowl of soup I knew she wouldn't eat. I could hear her snoozing in the recliner before I even got the dishes washed. I knew I should try to wake her, but couldn't bear the thought of the argument that would ensue.

Things were bad, really bad. They had been for some time. I had been warned they would be, but I suppose I had not completely accepted this until reality began closing the gap on my hope.

I had my moments of grief, panic, anger. They seemed to come in never-ending waves and I fought for my own sanity. I looked for normalcy in this new life with very little luck. I had done my best to continue doing the things I loved, but those things drifted further and further away each day. Even trips to the pharmacy or the grocery store were a hassle.

I poured a cup of coffee as my cell phone started to ring. I grabbed it, hoping it wouldn't wake her. The lady on the other end of the call began rattling off something about my expiring car warranty. I hung up without responding. I was too tired and needed some time alone without interruption. I powered down the phone and headed toward the back porch to read. I didn't even make it to the back door before I heard mother shuffling her feet as she made her way down the hall.

"I'd like to go to the park today," she said matter-of-factly. She continued to make plans for herself as if she had full ability.

"It's raining, Mom."

"I don't care. I want to go to the park, and I am going to the park. Where are my car keys?"

Mom didn't have a car. She hadn't driven in years, and no longer carried a valid driver's license. I had tried to explain this to her once before and was accused of holding her captive. She spent the next thirty minutes banging on the front window, begging the neighborhood children to help her escape. For weeks, I was asked about the lady in my prison. It wasn't easy explaining my life to a bunch of ten-year-olds. On the other hand, I learned a very valuable lesson that day: distraction.

"I'll look for the car keys while you get your shoes on. And don't forget a raincoat." Mom didn't own a raincoat, and I knew this would keep her busy until she forgot all about the park.

We didn't spend much time away from home anymore. I couldn't bear the thought of having an episode in public, not again. It was too difficult trying to explain away the fits and tantrums. No one seemed to understand what we were going through, and the harsh looks were more than I could stand.

Chapter Two

Sod Story

"Oh, for the love...why is he walking so slow?" I looked up from my book to see dad sauntering across the highway. In spite of the fast-approaching traffic, he didn't seem to be in a hurry. I saw the agitation setting on mom's face but I knew it came from a place of worry. Dad bent down just before he reached the median and scooped up his prize, holding it out at arm's length so as to not get his shirt dirty. He waited for another break in traffic before heading back toward the car.

"And just where do you plan on putting that?" Mom yelled out of the slightly cracked passenger window as she forced the butt of a cigarette out. Dad didn't hear her, but walked to the back of the car and opened the trunk.

"There's going to be dirt all over the trunk of my new car," Mom exclaimed. The sod hit the carpet with a thud and I realized just how heavy one square of lawn really was. It would take almost an entire year of picking up squares of sod dropped by flatbeds on their way to create landscaped masterpieces before Dad would be satisfied with our yard. Each time, we would drag the twelve by twelve square home, place it in the baldest spot of the yard, and water it until it started to take root and spread.

Dad slammed the trunk shut, completely out of breath. Mom turned her entire body toward the window in a dramatic display so Dad would know how upset she was about the trunk carpet. He didn't acknowledge her, even after several heavy, disapproving sighs. She finally corrected herself in her seat and lit up another cigarette. I sunk back into Charlotte's Web as Dad turned up the radio.

We were going to have lunch with my memaw and papaw. I was starving. It was Sunday afternoon, and they were "church folk" as my dad called it, which meant we didn't eat lunch until they got out of service. The cafeteria that they liked was almost forty minutes away. The drive was excruciating, and the food was mediocre, but Memaw let me push my own tray down the line and tell the ladies dawning hair nets what I wanted to eat. I always asked for the yellow cake with chocolate fudge icing. It was my favorite dessert, and I liked when the icing had a bit of crunch from undercooked sugar.

"Wow, that cake is almost as big as you are," the lady running the cash register at the end of the line said, way too loud. She threw her head back and cackled at her own joke. I wonder how many kids she had said this to already that day. Papaw picked up my tray and ignored my pleas to carry it myself since I "wasn't a baby anymore".

All the tables were taken, so we crowded into a booth. That meant I had to sit in a chair at the end, which made me feel like I was in the way of everyone that walked by. Memaw asked the waitress for a booster seat, but when my shoulders dropped with disappointment, she waved her away before she could get it to the table.

The adults made small talk, mostly about how hot of a summer it had been and whether the Tampa Bay Buccaneers were going to be any good that year. Memaw pulled a stick of gum out of her purse and handed it to me.

"Keep the wrapper on until you are finished eating."

She reached back in and pulled out a stack of papers. I instantly recognized them as the coloring sheets that they hand out in Sunday School class. I hadn't been able to go to church with them as much since we had moved to the next town over. Dad said it made more sense to live closer to his work, but I could tell Mom was sad. I loved our new house. It was much nicer than the trailer we had lived in and it felt cozy. The carpet was so much cleaner than the linoleum I was used to and sometimes I would slide out of bed at night and pull my blanket to the floor with me, just to lie on it. I would push all the fibers to one side and then pull my hands through it in the other direction to make stripes in the fabric. I even enjoyed vacuuming because of the lines the machine would leave behind as you moved from one side of the room to the other.

"So you still like the house, then?" I knew Memaw missed us being so close, but wanted Mom to be happy. Mom nodded her head with a mouth full of black-eyed peas. Memaw reached her hand out and patted Mom's hand.

"Good, I think it is a wonderful neighborhood."

Dad started rambling about his new job. He was proud to be making a little more money and went on and on about buying mom the new car.

"She's a beauty," he said proudly. "And less than 50,000 miles on her. It was a steal of a deal."

"Can't be good on gas, no sports car is," Papaw said disapprovingly.

Dad stuffed a whole half of a dinner roll in his mouth and looked over at mom. She leaned in and placed her head on his shoulder.

"Aw daddy, it's not that bad. I don't drive around much, anyway."

"You had to move all the way to another town to live just so you wouldn't have to drive around much. Now we don't see you as much and your momma always has to worry about you." He turned and looked at dad. "And what happens when you lose this job of yours? Where will you work then? And how are you going to pay for that Ford Mustang with no income? Construction work isn't consistent. They get rid of folks all the time."

Dad's hand made a hard fist and came down onto the table with a thud. I expected Dad to yell, but his face softened and he spoke gently.

"This company has been around for a long time. And they paid me a sign-on bonus to start with them right away. There's plenty of work."

"He's a hard worker, daddy. And that sign-on bonus got me a new car, so I'm happy." Mom smiled as she winked at Dad.

We finished our meal, and I begged for a quarter to spend at the gumball machine on the way out of the door. Dad said no, but Papaw slipped me his change when Dad went to the bathroom.

As we drove away that day, I sat on my knees in the backseat and watched my grandparents through the back window. Memaw pulled a wad of napkins from the restaurant out of her purse and handed them to Papaw. He unlocked her door and opened it for her to get in, placing the paper loot into the glove box. I remembered the stick of gum Memaw gave me- I had left it on the table at the restaurant. I wasn't upset about it though, I had used Papaw's change to buy a handful of M&M's and knew they would keep me busy most of the way home.

After that day, we didn't go there to eat anymore. I assumed it was because gas cost too much in mom's Mustang. Sometimes Memaw and Papaw would come by. I would run out to greet them and see if they brought presents. Mom would sit out on the porch with them until Papaw would say, "Welp, I guess we better mosey on back home." Mom would usually cry as soon as they were out of sight.

Dad stopped working at the construction company after several months of inconsistent work. Mom said he had to get a job with a forty-hour work week if he wanted her to be able to pay the bills. He did some odd jobs until he found a mechanic shop that was looking for somebody who could work on cars. Dad was always good with cars. We never had to take our own cars to the shop. Dad did all the work on them himself.

Not too long after mom got her new car, it was gone. It just disappeared one day to never return. I asked dad where it went and he told me it wasn't a good car for a family to drive. Getting rid of that car changed everything. Mom and dad fought about it constantly. Dad threw out my mom's favorite picture of herself in the driver's seat wearing a leather jacket. Dad started to worry all the time. He would pace the floor- mom would cry. Then my dad started to drink- and one day, mom stopped crying. She began to cater to dad and seemed to find a balance in making life easier for him. I accepted this new normal and before too long, it was hard to remember any other way. I didn't know to question things anymore. I assumed every other family looked exactly like ours. On the outside, we looked like everybody else and I couldn't begin to understand the unraveling that was taking place amongst the surrounding adults.

Chapter Three

Birthday Bike

I received a bicycle for my sixth birthday. It was one of the nice ones, with a banana seat, bright yellow paint, and black lettering; the inside of the tires were white. It was a gift from Aunt Margie, my mom's sister. Dad brought it home in the back of his truck.

Aunt Margie was my only aunt, and one of my favorite people. She was loud and full of energy. She didn't really care what people thought of her. She said whatever she wanted to say and did whatever seemed to make her happy. She told stories of her and mom growing up in "the sticks" — whatever that meant. She talked about being poor as a kid and living on a working farm. She recounted her days of milking cows and chasing chickens around the yard. She talked about how she would make fun of people in "fancy clothes" and said it was way more classy to wear clothes you had made yourself, anyway. She had never had a bike growing up and had begged mom to let her be the one to buy me my first.

"Time to learn to fly, sis," Dad said as he pulled it out of the back of his pickup truck.

It had a set of training wheels that he agreed I could keep on for a few days to give me some practice. Dad was always good about stuff like that. He knew how to push me just enough without pushing too hard. After fetching some tools from the shed out back, he checked the bike to make sure it was ready for riding. He tightened the bolts on the training wheels just to make sure I knew they were safe.

"Okay, you're all set!"

He had set up a boundary at the end of the driveway and told me not to cross it. He helped me onto the seat and showed me how to push the pedals backward to brake. He watched me pedal my way up to the house and back down to the road several times before heading inside. I made several laps on my own before dad emerged from the house with his beer and peanuts-plopping himself down in his usual spot on the porch.

"Faster, Lydia! Really make that thing fly," he cheered from behind the screen.

Before long, I could hear the effects of the beer dripping off of each word he spoke. But the need to make him proud propelled me on and I pedaled as fast as my short legs would allow.

As I neared the end of the driveway, I forgot just how much strength it took to push those pedals back enough to stop the bike with all the momentum my determination had pushed into it. The bike flew past the barrier made mostly of old paint cans and I found myself zooming across our road.

Dad shot up from his seat and flew out of the screen door toward me. My body tensed as I looked back and saw the anger in his eyes.

"Get off the bike, Lydia, and get in the house!"

I felt small as he towered over me and I left the bike on the road as I ran toward the safety of home. As I reached the front door, I looked back and saw a rage that my young mind simply could not comprehend. In all of dad's moments, I had never once felt like I was at the helm of his anger. This was new.

Things were never again as they had been that day before I made dad angry. He didn't seem to have the energy to play much anymore and tried less and less to make me laugh. Mom forced me to continue practicing riding without Dad by my side and eventually, after proving my talent on the bike, Dad removed the training wheels and allowed me to ride on the road. Slowly I watched him fade away as if being a dad had become too hard and he had chosen to punch the time clock on it.

At least he had taught me how to fly before he had let me go.

Chapter Four

Jimmy Bramble

Two weeks. That's how long it took Jimmy Bramble to ask me out. I'd never had a boyfriend before, so when he moved onto my street, I was on a mission. It was summer, and he was moving into the only house on the block with a swimming pool. He wasn't the cutest boy I knew, but he held the key to summer refreshment and, with any luck, would be my first kiss, giving me something to talk about upon my return to school as a fifth grader.

The day he moved in, I made an appearance. I knew if I was to have any luck at all, I would need to stop by for a visit before Abby got her preppy, no-good hands on him. I quickly threw on the prettiest sundress I could find, pulled my bicycle out of the garage, and headed his way.

"Be back before dinner," Mom yelled through the screen door as it slammed closed.

I played it cool, ribbons from my handlebars blowing in the wind, as I glided around the curve at the end of the circle. Jimmy was nowhere to be found. I stopped my bike in the shade of a large oak tree across the street and watched as movers unloaded large boxes from their truck into the garage. Along the edge of the outside wall were several gray crates, each with a name written on top. Tigger, BlueJay, Hermie, Pops, Tedra, Pooh, Barney Boy, and Edgar. I dropped my bike onto its side in the dirt and crossed the street to get a better look. Every single crate held a cat. Eight cats! I hadn't had eight cats in my entire lifetime, much less all at once. It turned out Jimmy's mom was somewhat of a collector. Jimmy said it was because his dad was a truck driver and was hardly ever home. His mom got so bored she would go get a new cat to keep her company while he was gone on long trips. I wondered just how many trips he took and why he would leave knowing that upon his return, he would find a new gray crate filled with a fluffy feline.

It wasn't long before I discovered Jimmy didn't handle his dad's occupation much better than his mom did. This was something I could not understand. I loved for my dad to be gone. Things were so much different when he wasn't around. Mom and I would sit and talk for hours, laughing and cutting up. She would let me in the kitchen to help with dinner and we would bake cookies to eat while we watched Jeopardy. Whenever mom and dad would make up, he would return and so would our dreadful way of life. Mom didn't laugh much with him around. She kept to herself and cleaned a lot. Dad spent most of his time out on the front porch eating peanuts and drinking beer. Every now and then, you would hear him yell for Mom.

"Irene, get me another beer, would ya?"

For the first couple of beers, he would ask politely, even throwing in a *'please'* for good measure. Several drinks into it, a much harsher tone rang in his voice.

"My beer is empty, Irene…" His voice would trail into an inaudible mutter… "Why God gave me a good-for-nothing wife…wasn't nothing till I gave her…the life…of a…."

He would eventually nod off and Mom would run out to put out his cigarette. Then she'd quietly sweep up the peanut shells so he wouldn't trip on them if he decided to get up for another beer.

"How come all your dad ever does is drink beer and eat peanuts?" Jimmy asked me one day.

I was embarrassed by the fact I had him around enough to notice.

"Cause he's a miserable fool, that's why."

I didn't really have an answer. I just assumed most adults hated their lives and had no idea how to cope. I had no idea what could have happened in life to make this man so hateful and terribly unhappy. All I knew was the best thing to do was stay out of his way. I never worried about my dad becoming physically violent, but sometimes the psychological damage is far worse than any damage left by bruises.

Jimmy ended up being my boyfriend for almost the whole year. We didn't act like boyfriend and girlfriend, although neither of us really knew what that meant anyway. We hung out a lot and played with his cats. I even watched as a ninth little bundle of furry joy,

Roscoe, was added to the mix after he mysteriously appeared at Jimmy's front door.

Well, maybe not so mysteriously. He might have been placed there quite intentionally.

You see, Jimmy and I spent many days up in a treehouse in his backyard. We would play house, although I am pretty sure Jimmy had no interest in being 'dad' to one of his mom's cats. But he played along anyway to keep me happy- I think he liked the company and knew I needed somewhere to hang out after school. One day in particular, we had left a can of cat food up in the treehouse and upon returning from a snack break, discovered an old, smelly cat had made its way up the branches and into our treehouse. He licked away at the empty can until he had pushed it right off the side of the treehouse floor. His fur was matted and smelled like garbage. Underneath his patchy fur, skin clung to a boney frame, and we knew he hadn't been fed in a while.

"Give him the rest of your sandwich," I said to Jimmy, who stood with three-quarters of a bologna sandwich gripped tight.

"No way! You give him yours."

"I can't," I explained. "Mine has mayonnaise- cats can't have mayonnaise."

Jimmy forced an oversized bite into his mouth and looked down at the hungry cat.

"Fine," he said as he hurled what was left toward the mangy cat.

The sandwich flew just over the cat's head, giving him a whiff of the meat by-product before sliding off the side of the treehouse floor and falling 20 feet into a pile of wood we planned to use to build a campfire once the sun went down. We both watched in horror as the stupid cat went right over the edge in pursuit of his half-eaten dinner. We ran to the edge and glanced down at the pile of wood, waiting for the cat to run out of the other side. Nothing. No movement at all.

"You stay here," Jimmy said.

"You're not the boss of me, Jimmy Bramble!" I hoped the attitude in my response was enough to hide the tears that threatened to spill from my eyes.

Jimmy made his way down the ladder and I watched as he began pulling pieces of wood and sticks off the pile, inspecting them for cat guts before tossing them onto the lawn. He slowly moved a large branch, much expecting to find a squished cat underneath, but was surprised to hear a low growl warning against touching the last of the sandwich as the cat devoured it without even chewing. As blood trickled down his nose and leaves stuck in his matted fur, we placed him onto the rug of Jimmy's front door. He rang the doorbell, and we ran to hide before his mom answered.

From that day on, I spent a lot of time at Jimmy's. His mom let me name the new cat, and I felt a responsibility to keep an eye on him. Plus, I really liked it at Jimmy's house.

I tried to keep Jimmy away from my house. I didn't want him to think we were weird or my dad drank too much. I made up as many excuses as I could.

"We can't play at my house; my mom is sick."

"Let's watch TV at your house; our TV is too small."

"I think my house might be haunted; we'll just hang out at yours."

I think Jimmy knew on some level things weren't okay at my house, but I am sure my erratic behavior caused him to imagine things were worse than they really were. I was afraid he was going to tell his parents bad things, so I went overboard with stories of good times. I made sure to mention the time my parents took me to the zoo and how they always made Christmas such a special time for me. I learned this from Mom. She always made excuses for dad and only told people the good stories. Trips taken when they were first married, gifts sent to her from overseas while he was serving with the military, dinners they had shared by candlelight. I listened intently to each word my mother spoke. I didn't get to see this side of my father. He had been a miserable drunk for as long as I could remember. I didn't even know if her stories were true, but I enjoyed listening to them and imagining a much happier time for her. That was when I decided I would stop at nothing to see my mom happy. I didn't know the magnitude of what that would take.

Chapter Five

First Job

I started working when I was 15. I walked almost a mile to the only dime store my little hometown had to offer. It was a grungy place that offered toiletries, 2 gas pumps, and old coffee. The bathroom walls were a permanent yellow from lack of proper cleaning and the entire building smelled like the cricket container that was kept in the back for fishermen to buy from. My boss's name was Charlene. She was short and stocky; her figure much like that of a man who had spent his entire life in the driver's seat of an 18-wheeler. She wore a white undershirt every day of her life with a pack of Camels rolled up in one of the sleeves. Her voice was low and she used words I didn't understand; words like Caty Wompus, britches, and whuppon.

"Don't talk to her, Lydia," my dad would warn me.

"Dad, I have to talk to her, she's my boss."

"You don't have to talk to anybody you don't want to talk to, smart-mouth."

"What's the big deal with me talking to her anyway?"

I really had no idea what the issue was. She was different from us and I just assumed he couldn't handle that. We hid our dysfunction and led others to believe we were better off than we really were. Charlene was uneducated and rough around the edges. She worked at a dime store and drove an old beat-up truck you'd expect to see a hound dog barrel out of the back of.

"She's a dike, Lydia. You know, a gay." He cracked open a beer and took a long gulp. I stood there, in shock. "That's something you don't want to catch, little missy."

I called my Aunt Margie. She's the one who introduced me to Charlene and convinced her to give me the job. She and Charlene were friends from high school and still liked to make fun of the people they didn't like from 9th grade.

"It's true," said Aunt Margie. "Most folks can't understand stuff like that so they just don't give her a chance."

I vowed that day to be a little nicer to Charlene and show her I wasn't like my father. I could only imagine the judgment she received from people who didn't understand her. She was nice and always ready to lend a hand, and even though I knew nothing of her life outside of the store, I was pretty sure she wasn't falling asleep on a screened-in front porch, cigarette in hand and failures on display for all the neighborhood to see.

Despite his hate for Charlene, dad spent time in that little store every day on his way to work at the mechanic shop. He would buy a cup of coffee that he would complain about the entire time he drank it.

"Who made this coffee, Lydia?"

"I did, dad."

"Lord-a-mercy girl. This is the worst tastin' coffee I ever drank."

He sat at a little table by the window and read the paper while watching everyone pump their gas and air up their tires. Eventually, he would roll up his paper and tuck it under his arm, stretch his legs, and grunt as he stood up, usually mumbling about the heat or the pollen. He would buy a bag of peanuts to take with him and would pre-pay for a second bag and a six-pack of beer for me to take home at the end of my shift.

He walked in the door every evening at 5 o'clock barking orders about what needed to be done around the house and shouting for his peanuts and beer. It was the same ritual each night; he would end up on the front porch cursing at the neighborhood kids who stepped on his well-manicured lawn, peanut shells scattered about, falling asleep, cigarette in hand, and the 11 o'clock news blaring on the small television he carted out from the den. Mom would clean up the mess and gently shake him awake; he would cuss at her all the way down the hall before collapsing in his bed. I would listen from inside the locked door of my bedroom, trying to stay out of his path so his mind wouldn't recollect that I even existed.

The day I turned 16, I begged mom to take me to get my driver's license. I imagined the freedom that would come with the ability to pick up and go anytime I wanted. I saw freedom in the open road, windows down, radio up, driving away from my problems at 55 mph. It took me three tries to pass my driver's test. After a year of holding a learner's license, I had still only been behind the wheel of a car a handful of times and most of those were with Charlene. She would let me drive her around the block near the store for practice. Her big pickup truck would jerk with each gear shift. I would close my eyes, shoulders tense, and wait for her to yell at me.

"It's alright, shugg." She would pat me on the head and smile. "You can't hurt this beast; she's a tough one."

Turned out my license did not equal freedom. It equaled phone calls from dad at one in the morning after he had stopped by the bar on the way home and the bartender had taken his keys. I would find him hanging halfway off of a barstool yelling racial slurs at a room full of people.

"You're going to get yourself killed one day, Dad."

"Driving doesn't require you to lecture me, little girl."

I would turn the lights off as we turned into the driveway, hoping not to wake mom. Grabbing Dad by the arm, I would guide him out of the car and into the house. He would kick off his shoes at the door and immediately trip over them as he stepped inside. He would curse at them as if they were the cause of his misery. Then he would curse at me for trying to keep him from falling as he stumbled down the hall.

One night in particular, dad was too wasted to even make it down the hall. He lay on the couch, his head hanging miserably off the side, drool forming in the corner of his mouth threatening its escape to the carpet below. I squatted down in front of him so my eyes met his. I sat there, silent. An angry silence. A sad silence. I wanted him to feel the pain I felt, to know the hurt he caused, to hear the inaudible screams of my heart. I refused to move, refused to back down. I stayed level with his gaze as if I could speak to him with glaring eyes. Eventually, he gave in to the oppressive stillness of the air and drifted off to sleep.

"I do love you, Dad." That would be the last time those words would come from my mouth.

As I got older, I started spending more time at friends' houses. I watched as other girls my age spent time with their moms, learning to cook and keep house. They would sit with their parents at the dinner table and talk about their day. I watched as dads gave them talks about which boys they needed to stay away from and taught them how to change a flat tire. I waited for their dads to shout for their peanuts and beer and retreat to the porch only returning for pee breaks and to projectile vomit their misery onto their families — but that never happened.

That was when I started to realize my life was not the norm. That was when I met Ben.

Chapter Six

Ben

The first time I saw him, he was walking along the fence line of the football field. He had a gym bag thrown over his shoulder and a football helmet hanging gracefully off of his left pinky. It swung with every step he took. As he moved closer to the bleachers where I was seated, I could see the chiseled signs that he definitely worked out. He stopped and sat on the bottom bleacher, a few rows down from where I was.

"Got a light?"

I froze as he peered up at me, the long cigarette hanging from his bottom lip threatening to fall to the ground with each syllable he spoke.

"Yeah."

He tossed his bag onto the seat and pulled a pack of Marlboros out of the side pocket. He held them up toward me, a gesture that seemed so natural, like we had known each other forever and shared cigarettes often. I got up and made my way down the steps to the bottom bleacher and pulled one from the pack. I had recently started taking cigarettes out of my dad's packs to carry around, but didn't really enjoy the act of smoking them. It had taken me several tries to master the art of inhaling without choking and I was so glad I had put in the practice, as if it had all been for this very moment.

He motioned for me to follow him around the side of the bleachers to the back where we would be out of sight of any nosey adults that might be walking by. We didn't say much- mostly just stood in silence turning our heads each time we blew smoke to keep from getting the smell on our clothes.

"Don't you work at the gas station?"

"Convenience store, yes."

He nodded as if to approve of my response.

"So, you play football?"

He kept his face toward the ground and shook his head.

"No- why do you ask?"

Confused, I pointed to the back of the bleacher where we were just sitting, where his helmet still sat.

"Helmet…"

He lifted his head slightly, cutting his eyes my way and for the first time, I realized how bright blue they were. A half smile tipped me off that he was joking and I instantly felt like an idiot. I played it off with an eye-roll.

"You're kinda cute," he said as he kicked the ground underneath him, a tiny cloud of dry dirt forming around his shoe.

I diverted my eyes just in case he looked my way- unsure of how to respond. Do I say thanks? I wasn't even sure how to feel about this revelation. Was I cute? Or kind of cute? It felt like an almost-compliment. It was like being thrown a buoy that was a little deflated.

We finished up and flicked the butts under the bleachers in front of us.

"See ya around," he said over his shoulder as he was walking away.

"Wait, what is your name?"

He turned to face me, a smile across his face.

"Ben."

He didn't ask my name. Maybe he already knew it. Or maybe he didn't really care. It didn't matter to me. He didn't have to know my name. I already had it in my mind that I would see that boy again- no matter what it took.

My Aunt Margie came for dinner that night. Mom loved it when she came over. When they were together, the house was loud and full of laughter. They didn't seem to talk much in between visits, but when Aunt Margie was there, you couldn't get a word in. They would sit on the floor of the back bedroom, old polaroids spread out across the carpet, and reminisce about their childhood. They told stories of Memaw and Papaw and how much they both despised growing up on a farm. They would consume a pot of coffee and as soon as dad headed out to the porch for the night, mom would pull out a bottle of wine saved just for my aunt's visit. It was the only time I saw my mom drink. She had quit smoking years prior but when they opened the wine, out came Aunt Margie's cigarettes, and they were easily mistaken for a couple of rebellious schoolgirls. I loved watching mom have fun. It was a rare occasion and I enjoyed getting to see that side of her.

It wouldn't be long before my dad walked out. I didn't really understand why he left. He had it made, mom catering to his every need. But I think he knew deep down that staying hurt her worse than leaving. I felt so numb to it all. I wasn't sad that he was gone. Aunt Margie came by more often to cheer mom up and she was so caught up in her own sadness that I could come and go as I pleased. That's when I started spending a lot more time with Ben.

I saw him at a party one night. He had come with Ashley Weatherford. I hated her. She was new to town and had already dated several of my guy friends. She was trading them out like cars at a buy-here, pay-here. I made sure he saw me and I made sure he knew that I knew he was with Ashley. I had spent most of the night following him around secretly waiting for him to stand near her so I could give a disapproving glare. I finally caught them standing in the kitchen, peering into the refrigerator together. I walked over and leaned in front of them, grabbing a beer from the door. I made eye contact with Ben and lingered for a moment, long enough to make it awkward. I made a beeline for Craig, a guy that I knew liked me and would hold a conversation long enough to, hopefully, make Ben jealous. It totally worked. Not even 10 minutes later Ben was standing behind me.

"Craig is a pothead."

I ignored him and continued munching on potato chips while watching the game of twister happening in the living room.

"Left hand, red."

Two people dropped to the floor, leaving only one person in the game. The Twister Champion.

"I don't like Ashley," he said. "She's just my ride."

I turned and stood on my tip-toes so I was at eye level with him.

"Why should I care?"

His gaze never left mine, but he lifted his head and blew my bangs out of my eyes.

"You should care. We shared a cigarette. We're bonded for life."

I rolled my eyes.

"We did not share a cigarette. You gave me one, you used my lighter, and we never spoke again."

He grabbed my hand and pulled me closer to him. I knew I would be the one driving him home that night. And I did.

From there, it was a blur. I spent all of my time wrapped up in Ben and trying to make it through high school. Graduation came and went. I spent several nights a week at a community college trying to make passing grades and working full time. I ended up dropping out my third year in. Ben and I set a date to be married. He wasn't a nice guy, and I knew I could do better but he seemed to fill a void that dad had left behind all those years ago and after our on-again, off-again relationship endured several breakups and grand-gesture makeups, I gave up on ever doing any better. He had finished college with a degree in marketing and had landed a job with one of the largest manufacturing companies in our county. Plus, mom seemed to really perk up at the thought of planning a wedding and it was nice to see her have purpose. If I could keep her happy, and Ben content, everything was going to be alright.

Chapter Seven

Letter From Dad

"**Y**our father wants to see you."

"My father? You talked to my father?"

Mom tossed a letter across the table. I opened it and read.

My dearest Lydia,

I have missed you dearly. I know I haven't been there for you. I left at a very delicate time in your life and for that I am sorry. I needed to get out, to clear my head, to make things right for myself before I could be anything for you. I want so much to see you. I have found love again. Her name is Gloria and she has encouraged me to reach out to you. I want you to meet her. I want you to meet her children. They are wonderful boys with a great future ahead of them. We want you to be an active part of our soon-to-be family. I hope you will consider joining us for dinner soon.

With all my love,

Dad

I turned over the envelope the letter was delivered in. It had a Lily Lake address. That was only miles from where we lived. My father had moved only a few miles away and had gotten his life together, but couldn't seem to drive 20 minutes to explain to Mom and me where he had gone when he walked out on us. Here he was wanting me to meet this new family he had sobered up for, while Mom and I struggled to make ends meet, waiting for his return.

My mind wandered back to the day dad left. It wasn't memorable. There wasn't a huge fight, fists flying, doors slamming. Mom was much more reserved than that. I had just gotten home from school. Dad was home. This was not the norm. I could hear their voices from outside the door but couldn't make out what they were saying. They were calm, carrying on what seemed to be a normal conversation you would expect to hear between husband and wife. When I walked through the door, they both fell silent and turned to face me.

Mom looked sad. Dad looked- normal, like he always did during the times he was sober. These moments were few and far between, but I loved them.

As a kid, these were the times we would throw a ball around in the backyard, sit at the dining room table with a 1,000-piece puzzle spread out before us, and watch Woody Woodpecker on Saturday mornings. Dad would wake me up just in time to hear the theme song blaring on the living room television. He'd have a bowl of milk ready with a box of my favorite cereal nearby. I would eat my cereal on a tv tray pushed up against the couch and dad and I would mimic the loud bird and his crazy antics. It was the only time we ate in the living room and I grew to love our tradition. But these moments together grew less and less over time. Mom started having to explain away the outbursts of rage my father would display all too often.

"He didn't have a good upbringing," she would say as an excuse for his behavior. "And you can't imagine what all he has been through."

I didn't speak to my dad the day he left. We hadn't passed one another in the morning before school and I simply had nothing to say when I got home. I passed by and spent most of the evening in my room. When I emerged at 8 o'clock, he wasn't there. Mother was hiding her tears in the kitchen. I grabbed the plate of dinner Mom had set out on the stove for me, looked at her without one ounce of pity in my eyes, and walked away. Assuming Dad was headed home from the store with a sack full of beer, I only wanted to hide out in my room for the night. Mom chose to stay in the madness of their marriage and for that, despite the tears, I had lost all sympathy.

If I could take back one day of my life, it would probably be that one. Maybe I would yell at my dad about his decision to leave or maybe I would beg him to stay for mom. I certainly would have held my mom's hand that night, allowed her to cry without apology, and tried to help her see this was for the better.

I spent many nights staring at that letter. I studied each word, trying to make it mean more than it probably did. Part of me wanted dad to be happy, but another part of me wanted him miserable. My mom had suffered for so many years, now it was his turn.

My wedding was fast approaching. I knew I wasn't ready for marriage and was pretty sure I wasn't in love with Ben but I also knew if I was going to have babies, I would need to get started soon.

"I have no interest in having kids, Lydia."

I was sure I could change his mind.

As I held the letter in my hand, I picked up the phone and instantly felt uneasy. I knew dad would want to know I was getting married, and I had put off contacting him long enough. I dialed each digit slowly and took a deep breath as I keyed in the last number.

Ring one....

Ring two....

Ring three....

I was about to slam down the receiver when I heard his voice.

"Hello…"

"Um, yea, hi…"

"Hi, can I help you?"

"Dad, it's me, Lydia."

I stated my name as if he had other daughters to confuse me with. I didn't know for sure that he didn't, so it wasn't that crazy of a thought. We talked for several minutes. He asked me about my job and told me about Gloria's sons. It hadn't worked out for them to be married as soon as he had hoped, but there was still talk of maybe one day. He seemed unhappy and for the first time in my life, I felt sad for him. For a moment, I forgot about all the pain he had caused and just ached over what could have been. He asked about Mom. I ignored his question. I didn't want him to know she was still the same sad, lonely person she had been the day he walked out. I wanted him to think she had moved on and was living a happier life with someone who truly loved her. I changed the subject by blurting out that I was getting married. It would be a small, private ceremony at the park in town. I asked him to come, and he promised he would.

He didn't.

Chapter Eight

Wedding Day

I had dreamt of this day so many times throughout my childhood. I would be dressed in a long, white gown with my hair pulled back except for a few strains that fell out of my veil, curls laying slightly on my cheeks. My soon-to-be husband would be waiting in the next room with anticipation and mom and dad would be by my side. But here I sat, alone in a dark, wood-covered room without my father present and mom so confused by the chaos that she chose to retreat to a small hallway to pray. She seemed so lost. All the preparations that had kept her busy were lost in the moment. It was as if she had set up a beautiful day of happiness but in the moment, couldn't find the happiness. I think she felt my hesitation. I felt sick- not with giddy, wedding day jitters but gut-wrenching horror knowing that I was probably not on the path that would bring about the joy I so longed for. Repressing the gloom, I pressed forward- and so did mom.

The ceremony was short- too short for me to come to my senses and bolt. I felt a surge of relief when it was over. It was as if I had missed the opportunity to flee and could now settle into the new reality that was now my life. Ben spent the day in a limbo of pleasing our guests and dragging me into this new happiness he had created for me. He seemed more interested in the show than the vows we had just spoken in front of the thirty-six people closest to us. Mom danced. She was proud, and I knew she had moved on from all the preparations that went into the day and now had her sights on the grandchildren that would follow.

The years after would only provide heartache as preg-nancy test after pregnancy test produced a negative result. Ben would grow increasingly distant, consumed with work, as he tried to distract himself from the unspoken disappointment that crept into our marriage. Mom eventually stopped asking about our plans to have children. She seemed to be struggling with her own issues as she started to show signs of a life that was too hard for her memory to keep up with. Little things, like finding her keys in the refrigerator, told me something was off. Doctor's visits didn't give us much hope. While we longed for it to be a normal, aging issue, we were told by doctors that the days ahead would be difficult.

Ben had very little patience for the fight for mom's memories. He filled his days with money-making opportunities and belittled the side jobs I took on to try to contribute to our household income.

Chapter Nine

Visiting Dad

I don't know why I did it, but I got in the car one day and drove over to Dad's house. I hadn't spoken to him since right before my wedding and I wanted answers. I had spoken my vows with an empty chair in the front row where he should have been. Mom was starting to show many more signs of being sick, my marriage was a disaster, and I suddenly wanted to know why he had left me to deal with this alone. I had watched as girls navigated their way through adulthood; pretending to have it all together, but only because they had their dads at their side ready to bail them out, give them advice, swoop in and clean their messes. I wanted that my entire life and the realization that I would never have that hit me like a ton of bricks. I couldn't even imagine the extent of where life would be taking me with Mom's illness, and I couldn't bear the thought of doing it alone.

As far as I knew, Dad had pulled it together, remarried, and become a gem of a human to everyone but Mom and me. I imagined him giving advice to his new sons who were now probably giving him the grandchildren I certainly wasn't. I wondered what they would be calling him. Grandpa? Papa? And if I did have a child, would he or she be expected to call him the same? His other grandchildren would be the ones to dictate what his own flesh-and-blood grandchildren would call him. That seemed unfair. Life had been unfair, but I had always heard my mom say how "Life's not fair."

I remembered well the first time I heard this phrase. I had entered a pageant in our hometown and Mom had spent hours on my hair and makeup. The second-hand store in town had provided a bright yellow sundress and with a little crinoline, a pageant dress was born. I rehearsed a dance that I would perform for the talent portion of the competition and fussed over how my nails looked with their dull, clear coat of paint.

"I thought I could paint my nails red."

I knew arguing wouldn't get me my way but at eleven, I still tried every time.

"You are not old enough for red polish. You know your dad would never let you out of the house with it."

I had heard the talk around school. I knew which girls would be competing and I knew what they planned to wear. All the other girls chatted about how they were having their nails done in a salon and how red polish was *all the rave* in Hollywood. It was true. I flipped through every issue I had of Teen Bop Magazine looking at the nails of the models that covered the pages. All red.

"I won't win with plain nails; the other girls will have an instant advantage, Mom. That's not fair."

"Life's not fair, missy. And the sooner you learn that the better off you'll be."

As I turned onto the road of my Dad's last known address, my heart was anxious. What would I say? How would he react? What was I expecting?

I pulled into the driveway and gave myself a pep-talk before starting the thirty-foot journey from my car to the front step that seemed so daunting. As I approached the porch, I saw a very familiar scene. Beer cans scattered around an old, beaten-up porch swing, and a mound of peanut shells underneath. I breathed deeply, closing my eyes, allowing the familiar smells to take me back to a time I cared not to revisit. With my head low, I made my way back to the car. I knew this was the last time I would pursue my dad.

I had to let this man go.

Chapter Ten

Move In Day

The day mom moved in was a relief. She had already fallen twice. Once, Sue Ellen from next door found her out by the rose bushes. She had gotten twisted up in the hose and had lost her footing.

"Glad she didn't fall into those thorns," Ms. Ellen would say with a disapproving head shake. "Might have scratched her up pretty good, huh?"

The second time she fell was in the laundry room. I found her when I went over for our morning coffee visit. We had decided to get together every morning at 8. This was mostly for my peace of mind, but also to remind her to take her pills. She was typically waiting for me by the front window. She would make eye contact as soon as I pulled into the drive and give the biggest wave, as though she was having to flag me down. She smiled the best smile each and every time I pulled up. She was truly happy to see me, which most days caused me only to feel a pang of guilt over my attitude of having to be there. It was a hassle, one which caused me to lose my job after I went in late one too many times.

"I'm sorry your mother is sick," my boss started. I then listened as he rambled for several minutes about schedules and integrity. I knew this would be my last lecture and I would need to stop by the unemployment office on the way home. I dreaded the conversation awaiting me later that evening. I knew Ben would be upset about it. He had plans to carry out, which wouldn't be easy without my financial contribution. My mother, however, took the news quite well.

"Does this mean you can visit more often?"

Our visits started out nice. Coffee, small talk. Sometimes she would fix pancakes or make toast. I would read the paper while she went on for 30 minutes about what had happened on her soaps the day before. It was during these times together I started noticing just how "off" things had become. Sometimes she would serve ketchup with biscuits or put salt out with the creamer for our coffee. She spoke less and less about her soaps and spent more time staring out the window that overlooked the backyard. Sometimes she was upset over misplaced items or would get angry when she couldn't think of the word she wanted to use in a sentence. I still played it off to her age.

This particular morning, she wasn't standing at the window. I figured she had probably forgotten about our morning ritual and began worrying about how much of my morning would be consumed with having to start the coffee myself and wait while she cooked the breakfast I knew she would insist on making for me. I walked toward the door, but still nothing. I knocked gently, not wanting to startle her if she was still sleeping. After several attempts, I pulled my spare key from my bag and began trying to push through the now-growing panic. I could hear her before I even got in the door. She must have heard my knocking and was calling out from the back of the house. I don't know how long she had been laying there on the cold, concrete floor of her laundry room but her skin was a deep shade of blue and she complained she couldn't feel her feet. I decided that day I was taking her home with me, regardless of what Ben had to say about it.

He was gone in a matter of months.

I really enjoyed having Mom there. On good days we talked and laughed. Sometimes I took her with me to the grocery store or to get ice cream. She loved sitting outside under the tree watching the neighborhood kids run up and down the road, some riding their bikes along the sidewalk. She would listen as they told her jokes and would always ask them about their grades. One day she insisted we ride into town to do some shopping. I gave in, it's not like I had a job for an excuse.

"I am going to teach those kids how to really have fun," was the only clue I got to the reason for our trip.

We stopped at the local dollar store and after several minutes, she came back out with a small plastic bag. When we arrived back home, she called over several of the children still outside playing and from the bag produced a box of chalk. She then drew a giant hopscotch right down the center of the road and began teaching them how to play. It was well after dark before I got Mom inside that night. She went on and on at dinner about how much fun she had. I loved days like those.

Good days were often really good days.

But bad days were often really bad days.

One, in particular, was the day Sarah came for a visit. Sarah was a sweet girl that lived a couple of blocks over. I met her mother, Jill, while taking an art class. We hit it off as we laughed over our dreadful paintings. Neither of us seemed to be any good at working with oil paints, but we were determined to leave with a finished piece, even if you couldn't quite make out what it was supposed to be. Jill was a sculptor, and I was a dabbler. She created beautiful pieces that won prizes in art competitions, while I threw together many failed attempts at DIY projects. We quickly became great friends as she was filled with talent and I had an art studio in my basement. We spent many hours trying new projects and working to perfect our art.

Jill and her husband were unable to have children, so after a few years of trying, they decided to adopt. I watched as they brought home Sarah, a bright child with a very grown-up outlook on life. She had been in and out of the foster care system for the first three years of her life and had now found her forever home. Jill was ecstatic and fell perfectly into her role as a mother. They fell in love with Sarah and knew they wanted to adopt more children, but before they had the chance, Jill's husband was killed in a car accident, leaving her a widow and a single mom. She was left to raise Sarah alone, so I stepped up and offered to help as much as I could. It was a joy having Sarah around.

"Aunt Lydia, you're my favorite," she would say.

One day I received a phone call from Jill. Her mother was ill and she needed to spend a few days out of town. I had started cleaning houses to make ends meet but had lost a couple of clients and knew the money Jill was offering would be helpful. I agreed to keep Sarah, even though I knew it would be difficult with my mom around. Sarah was six now and was, for the most part, self-sufficient. She had been around my mom enough to know things were a little off.

"Hey Grammie Irene," Sarah called out as she dragged her tiny suitcase behind her into the house.

Mom wasn't at all amused that she would be staying. She didn't really like for things to be different and was intolerant of sudden schedule changes. She also didn't like that Sarah would be sleeping in her room.

"There isn't enough room, she'll mess with my things."

I assured mom everything would be fine and she should go about her business like it was a normal day. Everything seemed to be going smoothly. Sarah learned to ignore mom's repeated questions and mom eventually stopped talking to her. Mom asked me several times who the little girl in the living room was and each time I answered, knowing the questions wouldn't stop.

"Who is that little girl in there?"

"Mom, that's Sarah. You remember Sarah, don't you? She lives nearby."

"That isn't Sarah. I don't even know a Sarah."

I would eventually give in and assure her I would get to work figuring out who the little girl was and why she was there. That seemed to satisfy her and she would wander off into another room. It wasn't long before the two of them were chatting like school girls. Sarah would tell mom all about her school friends and Mom would tell Sarah all about her girl scout troop. I waited for Sarah to tell her she was too old to be a girl scout but she seemed to understand more than what I had given her credit for as she played along and asked mom what her favorite girl scout activities were.

I was hesitant when they asked to go outside and sit under the tree, but I eventually gave in and sent them on their way. I sat on the front porch and watched as they talked and laughed. I wondered what it would be like for things to be different. As I sat, I imagined my house full of toys, and children running up and down the hall.

"Who let the cat in the house?" I would call out, looking at each of my children in an attempt to discover the guilty party. We would chase down the feline runaway trying to shoo him out of the back door. I was saddened at the thought that I would never hear the footsteps of a child stomping to her room or the slam of the kitchen cabinet as children plundered through looking for after-school snacks. I would never watch my mom play on the floor with her grandchildren or hear someone call after me using the term mommy. My thoughts were interrupted with Sarah, pulling on the screen door, and shouting for a glass of water.

"You want something to drink?"

"No," she exclaimed, "It's for Grammie Irene- she's choking on dirt."

I ran out to the bench where my mom was seated and sure enough, she was coughing and spitting- with a mouth full of dirt.

"What happened, Sarah?"

"I put some dirt and grass on a leaf and told her I made a taco." Sarah started to cry. "I didn't know she would actually eat it!"

I assured her it wasn't her fault and Grammie Irene would be just fine.

"Time to go in, Mom. We can sit outside again to-morrow."

She didn't even fight me this time.

Chapter Eleven

The Wanderer

I could hear mom outside my bedroom door. It wasn't locked, but as hard as she twisted away at the knob, she failed to turn it over enough for the door to open. This frightened me the first several times it happened. I felt like the defenseless victim in a horror movie, covers pulled over my head in hopes of hiding as a killer stood outside my bedroom, picking at the lock.

This had become a nightly ritual. She would sleep hard for the first couple of hours of the night and about the time I was ready to turn in, she was wide awake and full of energy. At first, I would get up and open the door, assuring her everything was fine, and guide her back to her own room. This never lasted long before she was back at the door again. Over time, I learned to ignore it. She wasn't distressed, just bored. I would listen as she paced up the hall, open the door of the small cabinet nestled at the end, and then slam it closed before pacing back down the hall toward the family room. Some nights, she did this a handful of times. Most nights, she did this for hours.

This particular night, she was much louder in her movements. They weren't as steady and her hands seemed to shake with panic as she pulled at the knob.

"Everything okay, Mom?"

She rattled off something I couldn't understand and began her trek back down the hall. Reluctantly, I got up to follow her. I found her in the family room. She had switched on the television to a documentary playing about WWII. Her eyes were wide as she watched images of Hitler standing before Nazi soldiers flash across the screen. Images of children, obviously starving, hands high in the air as they walked down dusty roads with guns pointed at their heads. Women cried as they walked past bodies piled high in ditches, obviously looking with dread for the face of a loved one, while large puffs of smoke rose from buildings in the background. Mom looked at me with tears in her eyes.

"I think my mom and dad are dead."

She was right, they were both dead. They both died shortly before my wedding. Memaw was 76, Papaw was 83. Memaw was the first to go when she died of a heart attack in late January. Papaw was lonely and didn't want to live without his beloved wife. As much as my mom wanted him to hold on, he died of a broken heart 8 months later. I felt so much sadness that year, not for losing my grandparents, but for my mom, who not only lost her parents but would never herself feel the love they shared between them.

"I saw them there, on the road. They were both killed." Her voice was broken with heartache as she stared at the bright, flickering screen. "They've been killed, Lydia. They're both dead."

Mom asked for her parents often. More recently, she had started to ask less about my dad and more about her parents. This was a relief for me. It is easier to explain away the absence of loving parents than a deadbeat husband who walked out on her.

When she first started asking for my dad was about the time she had a hard time recalling my name. Her life was moving backward, and she had moved just passed the point of my birth. She would look at me funny when I called her mom and pat me on the head like I was the crazy one. Then she would move about the house, calling for my dad.

"Dinner is ready, Ralph."

The sound of his name from her mouth was enough to send shivers down my spine. She had spent so many years of her life calling him for dinner only to have him lash out with hate. I knew there had to have been happy times somewhere along the way but the bad outweighed any good memories I had made up in my mind.

I tried being honest with her, telling her he had walked out many years prior and he wasn't coming back. This was devastating to her.

"Where did he go? Did I do something wrong? Oh, I have to find him."

She would pick up the phone and try to recall phone numbers.

"I have to call Mother. She'll know what to do."

"Mom, your mother died long ago. Don't you re-member?"

This would start a new level of overwhelming sadness and I watched as my mother grieved the loss of her husband and parents over and over again. Her doctor finally told me to stop telling her the truth. Instead, I was to tell her everyone had simply gone to the store as if they would return unharmed at any moment. I began to live my life between two worlds; the real one and a completely false one. It was difficult to know what stage of her past my mom was in and I often had to ask prompting questions to see where we were for the moment. Some days, I spoke of dad like he was in the other room and she scorned me for playing such a cruel joke.

"You know good and well your dad doesn't live here anymore, Lydia."

Other times, she tried to convince me she had never married.

Surely I'm not the only person on the planet going through this.

Chapter Twelve

Support Group

It was during the toughest of times that I reached out to a caregiver support group. I had no idea how valuable they would become throughout my walk with this disease. There were so many others going through the same things I was. It was here that I met William. Well, technically I met his father first. He approached me on my way into the building before my first meeting with the group. He was older than mom, and appeared very frail, but didn't seem to struggle with his words as she did. He spoke very 'matter-of-factly' as he told me I had parked too close to the line thus making it difficult for him to get out of his car.

"We aren't even parked beside her, Dad."

There he stood, tall, with gray specks in his hair that looked like they'd shown up too early. He was dressed in faded jeans and a dark t-shirt just tight enough to display the hard work he had obviously put in at the gym. He looked tired but handsome and I instantly regretted my decision to skip makeup. He gave me an apologetic look before opening the door for Mom and me.

"I'm William, and this grumpy guy is my dad, Frank." Without making eye contact with William, I nodded to Frank and said hello. His forehead wrinkled as he screwed his face into a frown to make known he was not yet ready to forgive my parking error.

We made our way into the building, and mom spotted the snack table right away.

"Please, help yourself to homemade cookies and beverages."

Standing at the front of the room was a petite woman in her late twenties. I wondered what her credentials for leading an Alzheimer's Support Group might be. I later discovered she had helped care for her grandmother who had died. She had gone on to get a degree in counseling and co-led the group with her grandfather, who she referred to as a *caregiving survivor*.

The first half of the meeting consisted of games and activities meant to stimulate the mind and encourage creativity. Mom and I worked on puzzles and made art. She seemed to be having a great time. I scanned the room and watched as the young interacted with the elderly and felt sadness over my resentment towards mom. She made things difficult at home and I had forgotten how to enjoy my time with her.

In the far corner, William coached his dad through a game of beanbag toss. I watched as he handed him the bags, his other hand placed firmly on his shoulder. He leaned in and spoke words to him that I couldn't hear but watched as Frank's face lit up with pride like a child receiving encouragement from his father. William raised his hands above his head for a double high-five as every single beanbag landed outside of the hula hoop they were meant to be thrown into.

"I don't think you're supposed to drink that." The fragile voice of an old man pulled me back into reality and I turned to see mom swallowing the last of the paint water.

"Mom, no!"

"It's non-toxic," the old, balding man said as he had probably seen the same thing done before.

"He's right, it isn't toxic. But it probably doesn't taste very good." The man's caregiver flashed me an empathetic smile and handed mom a napkin. She licked the napkin in an effort to remove the taste from her tongue.

"Want to try the bean bag toss with us?" William placed the bags into mom's hands and gave me a wink.

My face flushed at the realization he had watched the event unfold. The embarrassment was quickly followed by resentment that he felt the need to make his way across the room to rescue me. However, I was too tired to fight it and was grateful for a moment to pull myself back together.

Mom didn't hesitate for a moment before heading across the room toward William's dad.

"I'm just going to grab her a drink," I shouted at his back as he followed after mom.

"No hurry, we're fine."

I watched as several people joined the meeting without their elderly. They gathered at the refreshment table and watched as we all played games and cleaned up messes made by our grown toddlers.

"What's with the new people?" I asked William, trying not to be overheard.

"Oh, those folks are here for the second half of the meeting."

"Why only the second half?"

"They aren't able to bring their elderly with them. They're either too sick, living in a home, or they passed on and these folks are here to be a support to others."

It made me sad to think maybe one day I would be coming to these meetings without mom. *How much worse could she get?*

For the second part of the meeting, nurses came in to entertain the elderly while we were led down the hall to a smaller, more intimate room. I took note of the turns made and how to get back to mom should I need to.

Once we were seated in a circle of chairs, we were encouraged to introduce ourselves. Being new, I was given the choice to go first, which I agreed to just to get it over with.

"My name is Lydia. I am a caregiver for my mom."

"Hi Lydia," the counselor replied.

"Mom lives with me. She has been sick for several years now. I don't know exactly why I am here. Maybe just feeling alone in this, I guess."

I watched as every head in the room nodded with compassion and understanding.

"I don't always know what to do. I don't really know what's happening. It feels like a nightmare sometimes. But there are good days, too. So, I try to enjoy them as much as I can because I know one day..."

My voice trailed off as I felt the sting of tears hit the back of my eyes. William reached over and I felt his hand on top of mine.

"We've all been there for sure," he said before pulling his hand away.

Story after story was shared around that circle. From late-night wandering to loss of appetite, a call to 911 after a fall to a good day at the park. With each story, I felt a mixture of sadness and comfort as I found myself wanting to know more about each person in the room. But I waited patiently for the stories to make their way around the circle, finally landing on the one person I wanted to hear from the most.

William.

"Most of you know me, I'm William. I'm a caretaker for my dad. Dad is doing okay- good days and bad days. Most days he forgets who I am but he knows he has a son and talks about me often. He doesn't usually know where he is and is always looking for something familiar. We look through family photos a lot, that seems to help."

His eyes looked sad as he recalled what he was going through. He looked around the room, making eye contact with each person as he told his stories. He would nod to each person before moving on as if to comfort them but I wondered if maybe he needed the returning nod just as much.

He talked for another few minutes before casually throwing in a joke about never marrying. I wondered if it was a true attempt at humor or if he threw that in for me.

Not everything is about you, Lydia.

The meeting ended with a closing poem written by our caretaking survivor about his last days with his wife. With most of the circle in tears, I was glad distraction has spared me that same fate. I hurried out the door, worried mom might be upset without me around.

Down the hall, turn left, second door on the right.

"In a hurry?" I turned to find William making his way down the hall as quickly as I was. For a moment I wondered if he was worried about his dad too but as he reached me, he slowed his pace. I did too and realized it was me he had been hurrying after. I played it off to southern charm. He simply wanted to help me find the room as a payback for his father's previous insults.

"I completely lost track of time without mom there to make each second feel like an eternity."

As soon as the words escaped my mouth, guilt hit me like a ton of bricks and I worried about what he might think of me.

"Just between us, I come to these meetings for the forty-five minutes they take dad away."

A smile fell on his face and I found myself entranced by his dark eyes. After a moment he leaned towards me in an effort to break up the awkwardness and whispered, "And the homemade cookies, of course."

We made the left turn and I set my sights on the second door on the right.

And then I heard mom.

Panic grew until I felt my chest might explode. I knew mom would be upset over my absence, confused by the strange surroundings. I couldn't bear to imagine how she felt wondering where I was and when I'd be back. But as I rushed through the doorway, I saw mom and heard the sound again. It was a cackle! A laugh so loud she almost sounded like an injured animal. I looked to find the source of her entertainment and found William's dad, standing directly in front of her wearing one of the beanbags as a hat. His hands were extended like he was a tightrope walker in the circus and mom could barely compose herself before bursting out in laughter as the bag slid down the front of his face and onto the floor.

"Well dad, it looks like you're still great with the ladies." William shook his head and began picking up the fallen bags.

"I've found myself very tired all of a sudden," mom said.

"Grab your sweater, mom. It's time to go home."

William and Frank walked mom and me to the car.

"Maybe next time we can meet early for ice cream?"

I nodded and handed William an old art studio busi-ness card.

"That'd be great. Mom loves ice cream."

"It's a date then." I wondered if he meant he and I would be on a date or mom and Frank. Either way, I was happy to have some company.

William and I grew close throughout our time with the group. He and I would arrive early for the meetings, accumulating hours sitting on a bench in the park across the street watching my mom and his dad roam around together. We used the moments provided by the unusual play-dates to escape our reality and explore the thoughts of a normal life.

"Maybe we could go out sometime, for dinner, maybe?"

The question was always rhetorical as if he knew it wasn't a possibility but needed me to know he wished it was.

"Sure," I would answer. "Think we could find a babysitter?"

"I don't see why not! Who wouldn't want to spend the evening with those two?" He would nod towards our *children* who were usually pulling each other's hair or trying to con a child out of their ice cream.

We would laugh and change the subject, talking about the weather or our latest attempt at hiding pills in banana muffins. I loved the way his tired eyes squinted when he laughed. I looked forward to each week as we started meeting earlier and earlier.

Chapter Thirteen

Frank

Time with William became the thing I most looked forward to. It was comforting to know there was someone else dealing with the same hardships as I was and I began to fall in love with our time together. Frank became like a second child to me and there were even a couple of times that he would remember my name. Frank was docile and sweet. On our walks, he would find flowers to pick and would give them to mom. One day he approached me with a large weed that he had scooped up, roots still attached. He pushed my hair back away from my ear and placed the weed in my hair, dirt falling onto my shoulder.

"Dad, you're getting dirt in her hair," William informed.

"I love it, Frank," I said as I pushed the weed back further into my hair so it would stay. Frank grabbed my face with both hands, admiring his kind gift.

"Looks good on you, kid. You should wear it to school today."

I found the comment funny and looked for William to see if the confusion from his father made him sad but he didn't look sad at all. He just stood there, his eyes locked on the interaction between me and Frank. Our eyes locked and for a moment, time stood still, just him and I alone in the park sharing a moment that I never wanted to end. Frank turned and bent to pull up more weeds and William took the three steps that were between us with such purpose in each step. He touched the flower dangling from my ear and pulled his hand down so that it cupped my face. I pressed my check into the warmth of his strong hand. I felt safe with William, protected from the cruelty of my circumstances.

Mom called out for me, pulling me back into reality. We turned to find her holding a handful of weeds from Frank.

"We should plant these at home."

"Okay, mom- we'll try."

Time spent with William and Frank brought me newfound happiness. I felt like a schoolgirl with a crush on the new kid. And Frank became mom's new best friend each time they were reintroduced. They wouldn't remember one another, but once they started talking, it was like they picked up right where they left off. Sometimes they called each other by the wrong name. Sometimes they thought they had known each other during their childhoods. Sometimes they fought like brother and sister but always found forgiveness as soon as they forgot what they started fighting over in the first place.

Frank started getting sick more often and seemed to be declining quickly. He began refusing meals and was losing weight despite William forcing cans of Ensure into his hands. His skin became thin and clung tightly to his protruding bones. He wasn't able to attend many meetings anymore, so mom and I began visiting with him at William's house. His face would light up every time we came to visit, and he would stutter through a broken hello. Even as he became bedbound, he always made mom laugh. It was as if they shared a special bond through their sickness and while all other knowledge escaped them, they were keenly aware of that bond.

Those precious times together ended rather quickly when Frank passed away. Several of us from the group sat behind William at the funeral and watched as they lay a folded flag on his lap. William never cried. Instead, I saw relief. He and I stayed in contact after that, long talks on the phone, mainly. We even met for dinner a time or two but it wasn't long before it became easier to stay home. Mom would cause a scene anywhere she went.

"Look at that fat lady over there," she would announce loudly. "Can you believe how fat she is?"

"Mom, please, quiet down!"

"But she doesn't even fit in that chair. She needs a giant chair for that size rear end."

It was easier to stay home and order carry-out. William would come around every so often and bring pizza or Chinese food. I felt guilty for still having my mom when he had lost his dad and he felt guilty for having the freedom I hadn't seen in years. Conversations between us grew awkward, and after Mom got him confused with one of her high school sweethearts and caused us both quite a bit of embarrassment, I stopped inviting him over.

Who has time for happiness anyway?

Chapter Fourteen

Move Out Day

Sue. I really did like Sue. Her pigtails were falling, but the thick strands of yarn had held their golden yellow color all those years. I remember the year I got her; it was Christmas Eve, and I was six. I had asked Santa for a little sister for Christmas. Mom knew this was never to be, so she bought me Sue. She was wrapped in a handmade blanket, which I'm sure mom spent months knitting. Mom was never good at knitting, but considering the small holiday budget dad allowed her, she knew that would be the only way.

On that night, when I should have been sleeping, I snuck into the living room and found her nestled in an old apple crate underneath our tree. I loved her from the moment I saw her and didn't want to leave her alone, so I curled up under the tree alongside her and slept for the remainder of the night. Mom found us the next morning and asked me what I would name her. Still set on getting a sister, I felt mom should name her; it would be her 'baby' after all. She named her Suzanne, which I later shortened to Sue so I could spell it.

And there I was, all those years later, with Sue in hand, crying. For a moment I considered leaving the doll in the chest and only packing up the others, but was worried that mom would miss her.

"Where are you going, dear?"

Mom looked over at me with kind eyes. She walked around the family room, navigating her way through piles of clothes, stopping at the half-packed suitcase with concern in her eyes. I tried to get everything packed into the back of the car before her nap was over, but her erratic sleeping pattern had foiled my plan.

"Why are you leaving? Where are you going?"

Her sweet tone, mixed with worry, soon came with a hint of frustration. After trying the distraction method several times, I realized this time she was too focused to fall for it.

Mom was all I had, and I was all Mom had. We had grown so close over the years after dad left. We had the conversations I had longed for growing up. Mom would write out her recipes and underline all the special ingredients you should never leave out. We spent holidays together creating memories I had hoped to one day share with my children. Mom cried with me at the loss of a family friend and laughed at me the day I called her in hysterics because I lost the car in a crowded grocery store parking lot.

I loved having her so close, and I told her the day she moved in that living with me kept her from having to live in a nursing home. Guilt gripped my heart as I sat among the old luggage, breaking my promise. I hadn't wanted this, hadn't considered it, until the last time mom fell. We thought her hip was broken, and the doctor said it would surely happen again if she didn't have round-the-clock care. They were right, and I knew it; bath time was almost impossible, mom was no longer able to use the toilet, and she wandered the house constantly. I could no longer provide the care she needed and deep down, I knew she needed to be somewhere that could. Still, it seemed wrong. She had taken care of me my entire life, why wouldn't I do the same?

"To McDonald's, Mom. For lunch." She looked at me with some satisfaction and headed toward the car. Finally.

Seated across from my mother, I watched as she picked through a cheeseburger like it was something foreign. I missed her. I truly missed the good times. Even after she had gotten sick, we had good times. And I missed them immensely.

Later that day, as I sat alone in a house consumed with unfamiliar silence, I picked up the phone and dialed his number. Williams' voice was strong but comforting.

"You made the right choice, Lydy."

He assured me things wouldn't have gotten any easier. He told me to remember the good times at home with her and work on the new good times that would come with visits with her in her new home. Full-time care was what was best for her and with each word he spoke, my broken heart began to heal.

"Maybe now we can find time for that dinner," he joked.

"Yeah, I'd like that." And that was true. I wanted William in my life. I needed him. So I assured him I would make that a priority. But as much as I wanted to,

I just didn't. How could I move on with life and find happiness with mom living in misery?

Mom spent the next several months on a steady decline in that nursing home. For a couple of months, she tried to participate. She attended their church services and made a couple of friends over coffee and board games. Her best friend was her roommate; a lady named Jillian. She was an angry, bitter woman who loved spicy food and cursing. When the nurses refused to allow either, she would throw things across the room at the door as they hurried away. I tried to get Mom moved to a different room, but found them to be pretty fond of one another. They would sneak extra Jello packs from the lunch area and sit up for late-night snacks and funny stories. I never saw anyone visit with Jillian, and that made me sad, so I started to talk to her during my visits. Jillian had Alzheimer's as well and would often confuse me for someone from her past. One day, I stopped by on my way home from work and brought in the newspaper for her. She loved books, magazines, newspapers-anything with words. She never read them, but would look at any pictures she could find and make up her own story.

"Do you see this picture? The one of the boy in the hat."

She would then make up her own news about how the little boy had traveled to the moon. It was the first time anyone his age had made the journey. Mom would listen intently and smile with pride over the made-up accomplishment. They acted like school girls, complete with pranks on the nurses and after-hours giggling. They would leave each other notes on their pillows, most of them containing nothing more than scribbles. They would take turns pushing each other around in a wheelchair and sharing Bingo cards on game night. One day they decided to swipe the magazines from the front sitting area and make a collage, but the nurses quickly stopped them in their tracks. They were handed a box of crayons instead and were forced to draw their pictures. They had breakfast together, lunch together, and you could find them every evening in the dining room having their dinner and making television plans for the evening with expired copies of TV Guide. Each night, they had the same ritual. The nurses would make them turn out the lights, they would chat in the dark about things that made sense to no one but them, and the first one to get tired would call out, "Say goodnight, Gracie." "Goodnight, Gracie," returned the other. They truly made one another happy. They had an unbreakable bond. But I soon found out how cruel Alzheimer's disease can be. It can tear through a friendship like nothing else.

One particular day, Mom wasn't doing well. She had started talking less and less and the lack of being able to communicate was frustrating to her. I knew when Jillian started 'reading' one of her articles; mom wasn't going to be interested. Jillian saw a photo of the President at a Press Conference and started in with a story about how this man was in love with her. As she went on, Mom started moving around, trying to get up out of her seat. I went over and held her arm as she swayed her way to a stand and headed toward Jillian. Just as Jillian was wrapping up her story, mom grabbed the newspaper, rolled it up as tight as her arthritis-ridden hands could, and bopped Jillian on the head with it. Jillian wailed and wailed until a nurse came running in to see what was going on. That was the day the nursing home staff moved Mom down the hall to the Alzheimer's Unit, where patients went when their disease was far enough advanced that normal day-to-day interactions were impossible. They put her in a private room, but that didn't provide much privacy. The other patients wandered all times of the day and night and would enter mom's room thinking it was their own. Her clothes were taken by accident and on several occasions, she was kicked out of her own room by someone who had gotten turned around and swore it was their space. This is when mom stopped talking altogether. It wasn't long before she was completely bedridden and the decision was made to move her back out to a room on the main floor. I asked for her to be put back into the room with Jillian but was told they wouldn't be able to. Jillian already had a new roommate, and they felt mom needed to be closer to the nurses' station. Somewhere deep down, I had expected Mom would see Jillian and her old room and things would go back to the way they were before we had moved to the Alzheimer's Unit. Common sense told me that wasn't going to happen, but my heart wanted it so badly. A part of me died that day, but not Mom; she had been long gone by then.

Chapter Fifteen

Nursing Home Visitor

As the days went by, I found myself struggling to maintain my daily visits.

I could start going every other day. She wouldn't even know.

The visits had become more about overseeing mom's care than spending time with her. She could no longer eat, wasn't able to communicate, and couldn't move on her own. She only laid in a fetal position- every couple of hours being flipped over onto her other side. Lack of food caused her bones to protrude, covered only by a thin layer of pale skin. She no longer made eye contact. Her only communication was babbling; stuttering her way through the letters of the alphabet, her brain unable to put together actual words. I saw only frustration in her eyes until one day my cell phone started to ring. I had forgotten to turn off the volume, only remembering when the music started to play in my purse.

Mom's entire body stiffened and her eyes darted back and forth as if trying to decipher where the source of the sound was coming from. I allowed the song to continue. When the chorus played, *Wake Me Up Before You Go-Go*, I watched mom's lips begin to move. Unable to produce a sound, she seemed to simply mouth the word, *Go*, over and over.

I reconnected with my mom that day. I learned that when nothing else worked to evoke a response from her, music did. Every day I sang to her and every time, her lips would start to move as if she were trying to sing along but couldn't remember how to form the words or make sound come from within. She seemed to dance within her soul, a dance so large it dared to escape from her lips.

This new connection with mom renewed my resolve to visit with her daily. After a couple of nighttime visits, I decided to start going later in the day. The night nursing staff wasn't as thorough with mom's care and after a few times of finding her in bed without clothes and an adult diaper obviously lacking attention, I decided to stop being so consistent with my visiting hours. I began to enjoy these evening visits. Mom was more alert at night and seemed to enjoy my being there after a good day's rest. I would sing to her and she would look into my eyes with unspoken communication. I found comfort in this new routine. Like a mother tucking her child in for the night- but roles reversed. And even though this was not the norm, it was something we shared, and I began to be thankful for our crazy norm. We were bonded over circumstances others would never have the opportunity to experience.

One day, Jill and Sarah came to visit. They had gone to live with Jill's mom after Jill's husband died. I missed seeing her regularly but we stayed in touch and she was still my closest friend. We would spend hours on the phone catching up and she had been patient as she talked me through the heartache of missing William.

I hadn't seen her or Sarah in over a year and I was happy to have their company. They stayed with me since I now had a spare room where mom used to be. I moved my visits to see mom to an earlier time so Sarah could visit Grammie Irene without being out too late.

As we pulled into the parking lot, I thought I caught sight of William's truck pulling out. *Why would he be here?* As we entered the building, I pointed Jill and Sarah into mom's room and walked over to the nurse's station.

"Has mom had any visitors today?"

"Not sure about today, but there's a gentleman that comes by often."

"How often?"

"A couple of times a week. He comes during the lunch hour mostly."

She whirled around to face another nurse sitting at a desk behind her.

"Hey, Tom. Do you know the name of that guy that comes in here to visit Irene?"

"No. Nice guy though." He rolled his chair over so that he could see me.

"Sings to your mom a lot."

"He sings?" I asked.

"Yes ma'am. Can't carry a tune in a bucket, but he does it anyway."

I thought back to the times I had seen William interact with mom. They had bonded instantly and he had doted over her like he would have if she were his own mother. I had been so consumed with my own feelings I hadn't thought about how this might affect others who loved mom.

"Do me a favor," I said to them both. "Don't tell him I asked. Please."

Jill and Sarah visited mom with me every day that week. Sarah made her cards and her room was instantly brightened with construction paper flowers and pages from a Care Bears coloring book. I thought about William often after that. Each time I entered mom's room, I looked for clues that he'd been there and I never again passed by the building without looking for his vehicle.

Several times, a member of the staff would rush over as I walked in.

"Your mom had a visitor today," they would state.

I wondered how many of them knew about William and wondered if he ever talked to them about me.

Knowing mom had another visitor coming in freed me up to spend some of my visits with mom's old roommate, Jillian, without guilt. She was much more cognitive than mom and we were still able to have conversations, even if they were mostly about her dancing days on Broadway and other questionable stories. But, true or not, I enjoyed listening and felt I had a friend in her. A friend that required much work to attain after she would have forgotten me between visits.

I saw cards and flowers in Jillian's room one day and wondered who they had come from.

"She has a daughter out west. She's trying to get her moved out there," a nurse informed me.

She eventually did, and I lost Jillian forever.

Visits with mom continued as did my curiosity about William's visits.

I'm not sure what my motive was, but one day I brought a photo of mom, standing in the park with Frank. I taped it to the wall where Sarah's handmade cards hung. I wondered how William would feel seeing a picture of his dad, but hoped he would know that I still thought about his dad. I still thought about him, too. And I hoped he still thought about me.

The next day I came in to find the photo was missing. I couldn't comprehend why he would remove the picture of them. I let the thought bother me for a full week before calling him to find out why.

"It's nice to hear your voice, Lydia. I think about you all the time."

We made small talk for several minutes before I worked up the nerve to ask about the photo.

"I didn't take it, Lydia. I visited your mom a few months ago, but haven't been back since."

His response left me baffled.

Who's been visiting my mom?

Chapter Sixteen

The Inevitable

"Lydia." The nurse spoke softly as if her words could somehow form a pillowy buffer around my breaking heart.

I thought back to William, and how I had watched with a total loss for words as he handled each moment of his father's death with controlled deportment. His entire life had been lived with intent and purpose. He had chosen each step he took and demanded calmness in his surroundings. He was guarded but only in a way that would best serve him in times of hurt and sorrow; he was able to step forward and take control of any situation and make things seem so much easier than they were. He certainly wouldn't be sitting idle in the cold waiting area of a nursing home, hands weak as clenched fists grip tightly to the very chair he would need to get up from. But that was where I was. I found it difficult to fathom the idea of standing and walking into a room where I would speak my last words to my mother.

"I don't think you have much time remaining, Lydia."

Time.

Hard times.

The sum of them throughout the span of my life overwhelmed me and caused me to question my motive to keep going.

The time my best friend Lily moved away after her dad took a new job in another town. I sat in the backseat of our car on the ride home from school and I cried. Mom glanced into the rear-view mirror every few minutes but never said a word. She knew I just needed space to deal.

The time I had my heart broken at my first school dance. Billy Sanders had asked me to go. We planned to match my dress to his tie and Mom had spent an entire day searching all over for a dress that was "not too yellow, and not too orange." I arrived 'fashionably late' by about ten minutes too many. He had already started slow dancing with Jennifer Ward.

The time I found my dad lying face down on the wet grass along the walkway that led up to our house. I didn't know if he was dead or alive until I rolled him over and watched as the light seared his pale blue eyes, causing him to blink.

My thoughts were disrupted as two more nurses pushed past me and entered Mom's room. I shuffled my way to the door and peered inside.

The time I watched my uncle bleed to death from a self-inflicted gunshot wound. Blood in the back of his throat provoked a stifled cough as he drew in and released his last breath. I would spend years trying to suppress the memory.

The time William walked out of my front door for the last time. He told Mother goodbye and glanced back at me with such sadness in his eyes. Inside, every inch of my being silently screamed for him to stay, but I turned and walked away like I no longer cared.

Mom looked peaceful, almost too peaceful. I made my way to her side, leaned over, and kissed her on the forehead, relieved to see her draw in a breath.

"You should talk to her," the nurse prompted as she motioned for the other nurses to leave the room. "I'll be right outside the door if you need me."

Mom looked small. Fragile. Beautiful. Her eyes were closed, her mouth forming what looked to be a smile at the corners. As if she had a secret to tell but refused to give in to the temptation to do so. The thought made me chuckle.

"Oh, Mom," I slid myself onto the side of the bed and laid my head against hers. I could smell the familiar scent of her favorite shampoo. I placed my hand on hers and smiled at her bright red nail polish.

"The Lord is my Shepherd; I shall not want." I spoke the familiar verses as I had heard her do so many times before.

"He makes me lie down in green pastures; He leads me beside still waters. He restores my soul; He leads me in the paths of righteousness for His name's sake."

Time.

Good times.

The moments that hide themselves among the pains of life making it so easy to overlook them.

The time Mom checked me out of school on my birthday and made the afternoon magical with a trip to the mall to get my ears pierced. We spent the evening in the kitchen making homemade cupcakes with lard icing.

"Yea, though I walk through the valley of the shadow of death, I will fear no evil; For You are with me; Your rod and Your staff, they comfort me."

The time Dad drove us as far north as we could get without crossing the state line so we could chop down a Christmas tree the way he used to as a child. By the time we made it home, the wind from the ride on the interstate had blown off half of the needles. We spent the entire holiday laughing at our Charlie Brown tree.

"You prepare a table before me in the presence of my enemies; You anoint my head with oil; My cup runs over."

The time I took Mom to the zoo after she revealed she had never seen a giraffe in real life. We spent two hours in front of the giraffe exhibit before walking through every gift shop there to find the largest stuffed giraffe we could fit in the backseat of my car.

"Surely goodness and mercy shall follow me all the days of my life, and I will dwell in the house of the Lord Forever."

The time I visited mom after she was moved out of the Alzheimer's Unit. The move had caused her so much confu-sion and she didn't want me to leave at the end of the night.

I stayed until almost midnight hoping she would fall asleep so I could sneak away. She cried that night as I said goodbye and left her in the arms of a night shift nurse.

And there I was, crying through my final goodbye and leaving her in the arms of Jesus. Her final breath came with a peace I simply couldn't understand. It was as if she was moving onto something beautiful and had to leave the air of this world behind her. I saw rest in the face that was relieved of the spirit too big to live within its walls any longer.

I made my way to the front of the building, never to return. The sadness of it all weighed heavy on my heart, but I knew things were finally as they should be. I imagined my mom walking away from this world without looking back, without regret. Her eyes fixed on what was next- happier times, no sorrow. I didn't want anything different for her than her new freedom. Freedom from heartache and pain, sickness and confusion. For the first time, I realized why William looked so relieved when his dad died. He was finally able to say goodbye to the person who had left him years earlier. I turned to look back at the great big building one last time. "Goodbye, Mom. I love you."

I got into my car and reached for my cell phone. My heart was anxious as I dialed his number.

Chapter Seventeen

History Revealed

"Lydia?"

His voice instantly calmed me.

"Mom died today."

I heard him exhale as if he had been holding his breath since my name first appeared on his caller ID.

We sat in total silence, and I found myself resting in the comfort of his unspoken support.

No more would I have to worry over the choices I made in regard to mom's care. No more guilt over having left her in a nursing home. No more heartache because she no longer remembered who I was. She was finally in a place where she was free of the pains of this world and I was free to live a life that would make her proud. I didn't have to be the girl chasing after approval and affection from a deadbeat dad or the woman stuck trying to hold together a broken marriage. I was free to be who I wanted to be, not who my past defined me to be. I had my mother to thank for that. She had made me a strong person with the ability to pick myself up and move on with life. She had taught me what love was, and it was at that moment that I found it: absolutely and unconditionally in love with the man who sat on the phone, allowing me to give in to my grief.

William.

The next several days were all a blur. Family and friends stopped by with cards and flower arrangements bringing a surplus of casseroles and deli trays. Some kept themselves busy by cleaning up around the house while others sat with me and told stories of old times. A few of the men in the neighborhood came with rakes and hedge trimmers to help out with the yard work. I denied several offers to rid the house of mom's belongings.

Where were all these people when mom was sick?

"Lydi-lu, you home?" I smiled at the sight of my Aunt Margie as she poked her head in the front door.

"I'm here."

"Well, heavens to Betsy, sweet girl, you look awful!"

It was true. And Aunt Margie was always willing to tell you the truth.

"I brought some pictures. You'll need pictures for the funeral, dear."

I motioned for her to set them down and made my way toward the bathroom to check my reflection.

I did look awful.

I knew I'd need to pull it together, especially with William on his way over.

I ran my fingers through my hair and rummaged through the drawer in search of lipstick. After I came up empty-handed, I grabbed a tube of lipgloss, hoping its shine would give the appearance of some color.

That will have to do.

As I walked back to the living room, I stopped just before entering and watched my Aunt Margie. She was a few years older than mom but had the same soft eyes. The way she threw her head back when she laughed and pursed her lips when she was deep in thought all made me miss mom. They were so different in their personalities that I had missed their similarities. Now, when I needed so much to see my mom, I found comfort in the familiarity of my aunt's eyes.

She saw me in the doorway and patted the couch beside her.

"Come, sit with me."

She pulled photo after photo out of the box and had a story for each one.

There was a knock at the door, which didn't slow Margie down one bit. She pushed through her latest story uninterrupted as I opened the door to find William.

"Well, you sure are the prettiest thing I've seen today."

I placed my palm on his cheek.

"You're lying." I smiled in appreciation of the sentiment.

"Nope, it's true." He smiled and placed his hand over mine.

"Ya'll gonna stand out in the heat all day?" Aunt Margie summoned us in with one wave of her flabby arm. "I'd like to meet this gentleman you keep talking about."

I blushed, which caused her to beam with pride.

"William, this is my aunt, mom's sister."

William reached forward to shake hands but Aunt Margie quickly scooped him up into her arms in a bearhug. He looked surprised before falling into her welcoming gesture.

William took my place on the couch beside Margie.

"Look at this picture of Lydia when she was a baby."

Margie proudly displayed an old photograph of a naked two-year-old.

"Lydia, you were the cutest baby. Do you remember the time you ate the chocolate laxative out of my purse?" My Aunt Margie had an incredible gift for talking about the most inappropriate things at the most inappropriate times. "You pooped for days! Your momma was so worried."

Her hand disappeared into the box as she dug with purpose.

"I know it's in here somewhere…."

After a moment, her eyes lit up as she pulled out a tattered Polaroid. She handed it to me and watched intently as I held it in front of me. The photograph contained a young guy, early 20s. His dark, wispy hair was slightly out of place as he carried a petite, young blonde over his shoulder like a sack of potatoes. Her face was bright as she boasted a smile so large it caused her eyes to squint. Two people in love.

"It's your mom and dad."

I could certainly see mom and dad in their faces, but the smile they shared and the obvious joy of the moment was something foreign to me.

"Well, I guess there were happy times," I said as I tossed the photo back into the box and left for the kitchen.

After a moment, I felt hands on my shoulders.

"Lydia, you okay?"

I turned to face William.

"I'm just tired."

I was tired. Tired of looking for the good in a bad situation. Tired of making excuses for a father who didn't care enough to stick around. Tired of planning the funeral of the parent I wish wouldn't have died.

"Maybe you should rest."

"I'm just going to get something going for dinner. Just because I have no appetite doesn't mean these folks should go hungry."

"Tell ya what, you go lay down and I'll cook."

"You can cook?" I asked.

"Well, no. But I can use a microwave to heat up all these casseroles you've got in here."

I smiled as he turned me and guided me out of the kitchen.

"You go lay down. I'll make sure everyone is fed."

As I passed back through the living room, Aunt Margie flashed me a smile and pushed the box of photos into my arms.

"Your dad was a good man, Lydia."

I plopped down on the bed and set the box on the side table. I wasn't sleepy, just tired. I thought about the many journeys mom took up and down the hallway each night. I longed to hear the doorknob twisting as she rounded the end of the hall.

She'd love to look through a box of old photos.

I pulled the box onto the bed with me and began pulling out the contents. Beautiful memories perfectly encased in four by six squares held moments of happiness and bliss between my mother and father. I soon found myself digging through the top shelf of my closet, pulling out photos of my own to compare.

My photos displayed a completely different story. At first, a proud mom and dad bringing home their seven-pound four-ounce baby girl. My first birthday par-ty- a photo with dad wearing a smile and just as much cake as I was, Dad pushing me around on a plastic tricycle with pedals just out of my reach.

And then- nothing.

No more dad. No more happy, smiling couple. No more father-daughter photos making funny faces. I opened the bedroom door and called for Aunt Margie.

"Your photos differ from mine."

"What do you mean, dear?"

"Aunt Margie, mom and dad were happy."

"Oh, yes. They sure were. And so in love. They certainly hung each other's moon."

I stood, completely shaken by the words, not even sure if we were talking about the same two people.

"I never saw either of them happy."

"No, you wouldn't have. You were about four when things changed."

"What changed?"

Aunt Margie's countenance changed completely. It looked as though she were searching for words that would erase the last few minutes of our conversation.

"What changed, Aunt Margie?"

She walked past me and made her way over to the box. She lifted the contents, finding her way underneath them, pulling out a newspaper clipping from the bottom.

"Well, dear- something you were never told about."

I took the paper from her hand and began to read.

A Clinch County resident was found not guilty this morning by a jury in a case regarding vehicular homicide. Ralph Edwards of Shelbyville was being tried after his vehicle struck and killed a four-year-old girl on a bicycle.

At the corner of the page was a picture of dad. He looked young.

He looked broken.

That was the sad, pathetic look I had longed to see on his face my entire life and yet now it just hurt me to see it.

"The little girl shot out into the road and he just couldn't stop in time. He never could shake it, Lydia. He was never the same again. And to top it off, he had you at home- the same age as that girl. As he watched you grow up, he knew somewhere out there was a momma who was hurting without her little girl. So he drank. And your momma stood by her man."

Jill and Sarah came for the funeral. Sarah brought me a card with a picture of my mom drawn on the front in bright red crayon. On the inside were the words *Goodbye Grammie Irene.* I placed it gently into the casket that held my mother and nodded at the gentleman standing beside me, giving him the go-ahead to close my mother's casket.

"Goodbye, mom," I said as I walked away.

I wish dad would have been here for this.

Chapter Eighteen

The End

Two months had passed since mom's funeral. I had spent a lot of time trying to figure out who I was without her. Her death hadn't been about mourning her loss. I lost my mom long before them, a little more each day until she was almost unrecognizable as the mom I once knew. She had let go of everything that made her- her, until one day her broken body got so tired, it slowly uncoiled its hand and released its final grasp. It was a relief. She was finally free, and I knew as much as I missed her, I would never wish her to go back to that.

I had spent the last two months struggling with my identity outside of being my mom's caregiver. I had set aside everything else that mattered to me and zeroed in on her needs. When she was gone, I was left with nothing but broken friendships, no job, an empty art studio, and a void in my heart where William had once taken up residence.

My William.

The man who had come back into my life at a time when I needed him most. He had already walked a similar path with his dad and knew I'd come back to him when the time was right. He had given me the space I needed and had always kept me within his reach in order to be there for me when I needed him.

He had been the one to encourage me to start work on reopening my art studio.

He had been the one to pick me up and drive me to church each Sunday.

He had been the one to sit beside me in mom's closet as I went through her belongings.

And he had been the one that convinced me to come here- to mom's grave.

I hadn't been able to bring myself to come here. It was a place that represented a final goodbye to my mom and to the world we lived in together. And as hard as it was to see my mom's name on a cold, lifeless stone, it was harder seeing my father's name on a stone beside hers. The two grave markers represented a death to be spent side by side without the walk through life that most other couples share. My dad's stone also served as a reminder that he was still living and caused resentment in my heart that mom wasn't. She had worked hard her entire life and had served others until her body and mind were tired and rest was forced.

As we approached her final resting place, I took note of how clean her area was. I had expected half-dead flowers from her funeral would be scattered about and the weeds would have crept in, encouraged by the summer warmth. But that wasn't what I saw; instead, the ground was well kept. On each side of her stone stood large bouquets of my mom's favorite flowers- yellow and persimmon daisies. Sitting at the foot of her grave was a simple wooden bench. I ran my hand along the wood and noted the dark stain soaked into the grain that left it looking weathered and obviously handmade.

"Did you put this here?"

William shook his head as he joined me in admiring the handiwork.

I sat on the bench and faced my mom.

Sorry it's taken me so long.

I thought about my dad. He had made my mom happier than anyone else ever could, and he had broken her heart like no one else.

Aunt Margie told me stories of mom and dad, young love spurring them into early marriage and a blissful walk through the start of a new life together. Things had been as they should be for a young man and his sweet, young bride until that tragic day. I couldn't imagine the torment that must have consumed my dad as each day he fought against memories of the past, giving in to the guilt of stealing the life of an innocent child. I had so many unanswered questions and knowing my dad was alive and well *somewhere* left me mourning, not what could have been, but what still could be.

Would I ever be able to forgive my dad for the hurt he caused my mom?

Could we find common ground with mom no longer here?

Did he even care enough to allow healing in a relationship torn apart before it even had a chance?

I brushed these things out of my mind as I felt William's hand on my shoulder.

"Need a minute alone?" he asked.

"No, I'm ready to go home."

I laid a piece of chalk down in front of mom's stone.

In case there's hopscotch in Heaven.

I turned to leave, feeling at peace with what life had become. As I stepped past the bench, something underneath it caught my eye. As I knelt down, tears filled my eyes. Underneath the bench was evidence of a love I thought no longer existed.

Peanut shells.

www.ingramcontent.com/pod-product-compliance
Lightning Source LLC
Chambersburg PA
CBHW030006010826
48973CB00009B/2686